HOME PAGE
BY
SHIRLEY BASKETT

CONTENTS

Chapter One
INDIA

The graphics were awesome. Chad couldn't believe he had done so well. Even his younger brother thought the home page looked excellent. All Chad's favourite snapshots from the last holiday in Surfers Paradise had come out so well. They looked even better on the net. Chad's photo of himself with Nitty the rat, his favourite pet, was one of his best pictures. Nitty had his own page too.

So far he had thirty nine friends. Chad knew that was more than his friends had in the first few days of putting their pages up. Some had sent him messages and most were envious. None had a better home page than Chad Linders. He would not be surprised if people believed he was older than thirteen years, instead of his real age of eleven. His page was so cool.

Every time Chad looked at his site, more people had visited and asked to befriend him. He checked it every day to read posts and upload videos he liked. He checked his chat and sent messages to new friends all over the world that he had met on the net.

One day he opened his messages and there was a message that read:

"Hi Chad,
Your page has a photo of where I live on it.
India"

He didn't know this girl but he saw that she had some kind of contact with an aunt he had heard of in Australia. He went back into his page to see what the message was all about. There were three photos taken while in Surfer's Paradise that had tall apartment buildings in the background, but there were no houses. Chad, his brother Mike and his mother had stayed in one of the apartments just across the road from the main beach. They were holiday apartments and Chad could see no houses.

He sent a message back asking which picture had the house in it. A message came back the next day:

"I live on the eighth floor of the white building in the picture that has you, standing on one leg and poking out your tongue. It is the building with the dark brown colour running up the middle. We have a balcony and I can see the sliding door is open at our apartment, with the curtain half out of the door.

India"

This time Chad could see the apartment. He was quite excited. To think someone had visited his site and just happened to see their home. He wondered why this person was called India. He emailed back and asked how this came about.

"I call myself India because I like the name. That's my secret net name. My father doesn't like me using my real name. I don't think he likes my name very much."

Chad found that he could chat to India, they were both on Skype. India's father was on Skype and India seemed to be on her own a lot.

"Why do you think your dad doesn't like your name?"

"He's always called me Daisy. But last year, we went overseas to Hawaii and I picked up my passport and found that this wasn't my real name at all. He just laughed and said that he didn't like to use my birth name, he saw me as his 'Daisy'."

"What about your mum? Does she call you Daisy?"

"I don't have a mum. It's just Dad and me. He did have a girlfriend for a while, but I'm glad she's gone now."

"What happened to your mum?"

"We left her when I was little."

Chad understood these arrangements. "I just live with my mum and no Dad, so I guess that's sort of the same. I've got a younger brother, Mike. He's eight. I've never met my dad."

Chad didn't want to admit it as he had never really thought much of girls, but India seemed to be great to talk to. She didn't share his love of rugby league or cricket, but she did like pet rats. She loved finding things on the net and she dreamed of travelling to wonderful places, like tropical islands. Hawaii had been nice, but too crowded and she had to stay in the hotel room for hours, while her dad met business people.

India sent a picture to Chad of herself with her dad. She was just thirteen, but she looked older. Chad wondered if she really was thirteen or had said that to be able to create her page. She had a round face with dark brown coloured hair that grew bushy and sat on her shoulders like piles of wool. Her dad was tall and had the same type of hair but it was sandy blond. Chad knew that if he let his own blond hair get any longer it would go the same way. He tried to grow his hair once but it grew up and looked like a retro afro hairdo. India's hair didn't look too bad since she was a girl.

Then a week went by and two, but India didn't respond to any messages. Chad thought she had found something else to do or someone else to talk to and he forgot about her. Then one day he checked his emails and there was a quick note from India. It was from a different address.

"I'm sorry I haven't talked for a while. We've shifted. We shift a lot. Only this time, Dad saw that I was talking to you and was really angry. He said I wasn't allowed to talk to people from New Zealand, especially people from Auckland! How was I to know that? Anyway, I can't see what the problem is and since he won't tell me, I've found a friend who'll let me use her computer. I probably won't be able to chat. I hope Nitty the rat is OK.

Dad seems to have found another 'friend'. I hate her. She is sneaky. She only wants Dad because he makes a lot of money. He can't see it. She's all smarmy to Dad and behind his back gives me the 'evils'. Here's a picture of our new apartment."

The picture showed another high-rise white building with embellishments on the roof that made it look like something from Arabia. Domes and curled decorations gleamed white in the Queensland sun.

At the bottom was a café and shops. It looked to be right in town. Chad couldn't help but notice a man sitting at a table looking straight at him. The man had the ugliest face he had ever seen. He was glaring at whoever had taken the photo. He was wearing a black shirt, but his arm revealed a tattoo. Chad couldn't see what the tattoo was in the photo but it was big and ran down his arm, from the top of his muscle shirt, almost to his elbow. The man was bald but had a dark line of a moustache across his grim top lip.

Chad felt sorry for India but he had troubles of his own. Mike was going to have to go into hospital to have a major operation. He had been born with a hip problem and now he was old enough for some corrective surgery. Chad's mother was going to have to spend days with him in hospital and then needed time to nurse him at home for a few weeks. She thought it would be best if Chad go to stay with an uncle for two weeks. It was school holidays so he would be able to have the whole time away.

Chad was a bit afraid of going to his uncle. He had only ever met Uncle Gordon once and what he remembered was a grumpy, loud-mouthed man with a bristling stubbly beard. Uncle Gordon had never stayed anywhere very long, working in engineering companies, on oil rigs, out on strange projects all over the world. Now he was in Fiji working in a cane-processing factory. He had married a local woman and had settled in the tropical town of Nadi.

When Uncle Gordon invited Chad, it had seemed a good idea. Gordon must have settled down by now, Chad's mother comforted. He had a wife and it would be a wonderful experience for Chad to see another culture. He would be able to swim and have a great holiday in the sun. Uncle Gordon was willing to pay the airfare so it was done. Chad was going on his own to grumpy Gordon's.

9

India couldn't believe Chad's message. She too was being sent away. Her father wanted some time with Stacey. India knew Stacey had talked him into the plan. India too was going to Fiji. Her dad had arranged for his secretary to take India to a luxury resort for a week. India quite liked her dad's secretary Sharon; she often talked to her for hours while waiting for her dad to finish work. The only drawback was that Sharon was going to bring her boyfriend. India knew that this meant she would be lonely in the big resort hotel. She would have her own room and couldn't even talk to Sharon at night.

Chad didn't know if the resort was anywhere near where he was going to be. India didn't know when she was going. Chad was leaving in three days time. He said goodbye to India and wished her a good holiday. She wished him one too; but he was worried.

Chapter two
THE GARDEN

Mothers always fussed too much, Chad thought. His mother had packed everything he owned apart from Nitty. Another friend had to look after Nitty. His mother had fretted all the way to the airport and then looked sad as Chad walked through to the customs area. He was feeling a lot happier about this part of the trip.

The flight was great. He loved take off and landing. He ate everything on the tray and was very pleased that he had been given a window seat. He could see the clouds below him, hills and towers of mist and vapour. Too soon, he landed in Nadi. His uncle was waiting for him. He even looked very happy to see Chad. He grabbed the suitcase and hurried, talking loudly about how glad he was to see the 'boy'. They left the airport building and Chad was enveloped in the heat of the Pacific Island.

Uncle Gordon's house was not far from the airport. They were there in about ten minutes. It was down a road that led inland. The house was set on its own in a wilderness of tropical weed and trees. It was a bit run down and old and inside was dark and a little musty. Chad's room was just off the living room. It had a single bed and an old set of drawers; nothing else.

Uncle Gordon introduced his wife. She was tall too, almost as tall as Uncle Gordon. She was Fijian. Her face was quite long and fine-featured and her skin dusky and dark. Her eyes were gentle and dreamy. It was hard for Chad to know what she was thinking of him. When she smiled her mouth stretched wide and in the front of her white teeth, one tooth glinted with a gold cap. Her hair was cut short and sat on her head like a round black beret.

Uncle Gordon was almost delirious with fun and in high spirits. Chad relaxed; he hadn't seen his uncle like this. Perhaps he had changed. Chad related all the family news and Uncle Gordon laughed loud, roaring laughs. Haw haw haw! The laugh made Chad laugh as well. Aunt Sarai just sat and smiled occasionally. She was busy sewing.

Chad's uncle asked many questions about the family, but one question Chad found himself a bit annoyed with.

"Does your mum ever talk about your dad?"

"Not really."

"Little wonder. He was lazy too. S'ppose you still don't make your own bed?"

Aunt Sa looked up from her sewing and fixed her eyes on Gordon. She shook her head slightly and focussed back on her work.

Gordon stared at Chad for so long he began to feel uncomfortable. He preferred his uncle as he had been an hour ago. "Don't s'ppose she's told you about what happened?"

"No. That is, I don't think so. Well, I know dad left when I was little…"

"Didn't tell you anything about the hell he put your mother through?"

"I know she was sad."

"Didn't tell you about *her*?"

12

"Her? Maybe dad found someone else? Mum never said."

Gordon relaxed a bit. "Didn't think so!" He announced triumphantly and then speaking almost as if to himself added, "The kid doesn't even know about *her*. It'll come out. These things have a way of coming out. It'll come out in the wash sometime."

Chad didn't want to pry. He knew his mother had some very painful rooms in her heart that he never wanted to look into. Sometimes he heard her crying and she never knew he had heard.

The morning came and Chad was woken by the sound of roosters crowing before the dawn. He could hear someone up moving about in the house. He had found it hard to sleep on his first night in Fiji. It was so hot. Even without the sheet over him, he could hardly escape the heat in his small room. There were strange noises in the night and some sounded like they were in his room, scuttling noises, the shrill chirping of some sort of insect or bird. He yawned and got up.

Before he could open his eyes properly his uncle barked at him. "Good. You should be up early too! We have work to do. I'm mighty glad you are up here boy. I need your help. With all the hours I put in to my job, I can't get things done around here. I want to clear the garden to make room for some sheds. How can I be expected to do this with my rheumatic arms?"

Chad had forgotten the list of ailments that his uncle had nurtured as long as anyone in the family could remember.

"Get this into you. You'll need a bit of energy to work in this heat." He looked at Chad still yawning and trying to understand what his uncle wanted him to do. "Thought you could come up and laze around did you? You get enough holidays! I know your mother spoils you two. Well," his eyes narrowed, "don't expect to get pampered here. I plan to make a man out of you yet!"

Chad was awake now and nervously took the bread offered to him. It had jam on it but no butter. He thought to ask but then thought better of it. His younger memories of 'bawling-out-lectures' from his uncle started to resurface. He nibbled at the bread and tried to swallow it.

Aunt Sa came into the kitchen and smiled at Chad. "You want a cool drink?"

He nodded and she poured him a glass of pineapple juice. It was delicious and Chad gratefully accepted a second.

"Don't let me see you pouring that expensive juice down the kid's throat again," threatened Gordon in a low growl. "He can have water."

As soon as Chad had finished eating, his uncle led him outside. "You see this rubbish?" His hand waved over a heap of rotting sacking, bottles, tins and old bits from some machine. "Get rid of it. Pick it up and put it into these sacks here. We'll take them and dump them later." Uncle Gordon kicked a bottle and spat into the heap that Chad was expected to pick up with his hands. "When you've finished that, you can start on the garden."

"Garden?" Wondered Chad out loud. Where was the garden? All he could see was jungle.

"You're not used to hard work are you boy?" Sneered Gordon. Any sign of fun and laughter

14

was a distant dream. He grabbed Chad's arm, hard. Chad winced but turned his head; he wasn't going to give Gordon another chance to ridicule him. "All this is the garden! Get it! You have two weeks so that should keep you busy!" Then because it was his own joke he threw back his head, releasing Chad's arm with a "haw haw!"

There was one area he was not to go near on strict orders. Chad had no intention of going near those big dark metal boxes. They were stacked in rows behind the house, slightly rusted, painted brown and sealed with clamps of metal.

Chad had no choice. He was his uncle's prisoner. He set to work, trying to remember where his uncle had spat. He had cleared everything into the sacks in an hour but he was hot. He looked longingly toward the house. As if he had given a signal, Sa came out with a glass of juice. He hurried to her and drank it thankfully. He hoped his uncle wouldn't catch him being given 'precious' juice.

He looked about at the mangle of vines and roots. This would take longer than two weeks, he was sure. But he was also sure that his uncle would not let up until it was all done. There was nothing for it but to start somewhere and try to make a clearing around the house. He stopped often with a startle as some huge bug or beetle emerged from under a leaf or piece of wood.

He didn't know if these Fiji bugs stung or bit or would fly in his face. Once he heard his uncle laughing and saw him out of the corner of his eye, watching as Chad jumped, having seen the biggest cockroach he had ever encountered. He pretended not to have noticed Gordon because

15

he knew that things would just get worse. The bruise on his arm was starting to come out from the vice-like grip that Gordon had held him with earlier. Chad didn't want to give his uncle any more opportunity.

Sa called Chad in for lunch. By this time he was feeling ill in the heat. She gave him several long drinks of water and even Gordon said he could rest up for an hour or so.

"You have to drink a lot when you are working in the heat." Sa said kindly. "You will get sick if you don't. Now you come in and I will give you more water whenever you want it."

"Stupid boy!" Said Gordon and he spat out the window onto the deck. "Doesn't know the first thing about work. I could tell him about what it is to work! Lazy like his dad."

Chad could hear his mother's voice before he left New Zealand, drawing a picture of the holiday he was to have. "Beautiful white sandy beaches, you'll be in the sun and the sea to your heart's content." There was no sea here, just a sea of green and dirt and the salt of his sweat in his eyes.

It seemed like much shorter than an hour, when Gordon sent him back to work. Not long after this a car came up the long driveway, grinding up the two furrows of clay that was the road to the house. Two men got out. One was a Fijian, big and a little paunchy. The other was an olive skinned man with a bald head and a moustache in a thin line, over a thin mouth. He was wearing a black T-shirt and as he turned, Chad saw a massive tattoo that reached almost to his elbow.

Chad tried not to stare, but he had seen this man somewhere before. He couldn't remember. He was getting too tired. The man glanced over at Chad, and then with the Fijian man, strode into the house. Chad didn't like this bald man. He would make a bad enemy. His arms were tight and muscled and even in this heat, he wore hard black work boots. Gordon greeted him with a boisterous clap on the shoulder. The men went into the house.

It was a relief later in the afternoon to see the three of them leave in the old white, rusted car that Baldy had arrived in. The last words from Chad's uncle were as he called up the driveway. "See you don't stop because I've gone out boy! I know how much you have done so far and how much you should have done at the end of a good day's work!"

Chad worked on this fear for another hour but he could work no longer. His arms and back ached and he was starting to feel shaky. Sa came and rescued him and took him into the house in the mid afternoon.

"Forget his threats. He's all talk." She comforted. She brought the juice out again and handed a tall glass to Chad. Even though she was tall and not slim, she moved with such grace and quietness. Chad wanted to say, "What do you see in my uncle?" But he kept quiet.

Late in the afternoon he heard a car at the bottom of the driveway and stiffened.

"Don't be afraid." Said Sa. "He won't be back. He's gone to drink kava with his friends. He will come back late tonight. He will sleep late tomorrow because it is Sunday and I go to

17

church. If he wakes too early, I might try to take him to church, so he will sleep late. I can take you to church tomorrow too." She winked.

"Yes, please." Said Chad, never thinking church would sound like such a good option. His body was sore all over. He showered under the cold water, as the house didn't have hot water. It didn't matter, it was refreshing and cool and he felt good for the first time in the day. He fell onto his bed and slept, not caring about the heat, the bugs or the noises. He dreamed of miles and miles of jungle and vines and pools of spit that he kept standing in.

He nearly slept through the crowing of the rooster and realised that he hadn't even heard his uncle come home. That was a relief. He crept around getting dressed incase his uncle arose and stopped him from going with Sa. He was still aching and he didn't think his arms would ever come right again. How could he go on for another two weeks like this? No, now it was one week and six days. He was counting off his sentence.

They walked down the drive and on to the road. They walked along the main road for a time then turned into another side road that had tall sugar cane on either side.

"This is my church. It is an Indian church, but I like it. I go here because it's close and they have meetings in the afternoon and evening. I can go out all Sunday if I want to."

Chad understood little of the meeting. The singing was loud and the children sat so attentively. He wondered if they did this when they were at school. It was never like this at home. They all smiled at this blond boy in their midst and chatted at a hundred miles an hour after the service. He felt like a hero. They all wanted to know about his life and what it was like in New Zealand.

True to Sa's promise, they visited church people and stayed at meetings in the afternoon and through into the night. Chad learned to eat curry with his fingers. He loved the pungent flavours, especially the tomato chutney. As the day wore on Chad was starting to tire. He didn't know the songs they sung for hours and he was still sore from his work. As the dark came, he feared the next morning.

Uncle Gordon said nothing when they returned, except to remind Chad that he had work in the morning. He had been making progress too slowly. He wanted to see more cleared tomorrow. With relief, Chad realised that his uncle was going to work early in the morning and wouldn't be home until mid afternoon. At least he could escape the laughter. He was sad to learn that his aunt worked too and that she would be gone by mid morning and back later than his uncle. He felt safer knowing she was around.

Chapter Three
THE ESCAPE

He slept well to begin with but then woke in the early hours and tossed and turned, feeling homesick. He hoped Mike had come through his operation ok. He would be kinder to his little brother and would stop teasingly calling him 'unlikey Mikey' in the future.

He must have fallen asleep again because suddenly he was woken by the sound of a car leaving. It was the old white car with the Fijian. Chad saw it as it rolled over the last clay hill in the driveway. He was gone. The tyrant was gone at least for some hours.

Sa was up and making breakfast. She sat Chad down and fed him a stack of fresh pancakes with syrup and piles of paw paw and banana. He knew she hadn't started making these until after Gordon had gone. He hoped she wouldn't get into any trouble feeding 'the boy' pancakes. They washed up the dishes and Sa made Chad laugh. She was the only light in the house. He couldn't bear to think she was going to work very soon.

A pickup truck rumbled up the driveway. Chad was just fixing on his sneakers. He was worrying because his mother had packed him all his good clothes. These shorts were new and the T-shirt was white apart from the picture on the front. How long would it remain white with the work he had to do? He looked out at the truck. Another tall Fijian man sat in the driver's seat. He was fiddling with the dashboard. He didn't see Chad.

Aunt Sa was getting something from the bedroom, so Chad wandered out onto the driveway. The truck had an open tray on the back with a tarpaulin bunched in a heap in one corner. Chad almost caught his breath. He looked back hurriedly toward the house but couldn't see a sign of his aunt. Without weighing it up, he hauled himself quickly onto the back of the truck and crawled as fast as he could toward the tarpaulin. He had just pulled it over him when he heard the front door shut. He could see through a small tear in the cloth. His aunt was looking about the garden. She called out, "Chad, see you later! Don't work too hard!" She walked briskly to the truck and jumped into the passenger side. As she shut the door he heard her say, "My nephew. I don't know where he has gone, but I am sure he'll be ok."

Chad watched through the hole and could see the two through the cab window. The driver shrugged and looked casually toward the house. He turned the key and the truck moved out down the driveway. Chad's heart thumped. What would happen when his uncle got home tonight? He felt a surge of anger. He didn't care right now. He would stay with his aunt. She would protect him. But in his mind he knew that his uncle could be violent. He would have to pretend he had been sick all day or something.

There were trucks and cars and everyone seemed to be going in to town. He didn't know where his aunt worked. His plan had been to get out at the other end and beg to stay with her for the day, until she had to go home. The more he thought as he bumped along getting sticky and hot under the tarpaulin, the more he decided she might find some way to send him back to the house.

Soon the truck slowed and Chad could see a guardhouse. His heart skipped a beat – he would be found out! But the truck just kept moving over the speed humps and he saw the guard wave a leisurely greeting as the truck moved on. The gardens here were groomed and not one blade or renegade vine reached out onto the road, or the paths that wound past palms and hibiscus bushes.

The truck went around some large buildings and stopped. Both his aunt and the driver got out. The driver must work in this place too. He waited until he could see the two had gone out of sight, and then he emerged from his hiding place and jumped onto the concrete of the parking area.

He would think about finding his aunt a little later, when it was too late for him to be sent back. But for now, he wanted to explore. It was a hotel, sprawling in long arms of rooms with a central area for the restaurant and bars. He wandered into the shade, admiring the gardens. He had never appreciated gardens until now. The leaves of flame coloured shrubs and elephant eared vines were fascinating.

Chad rounded into the main part of the hotel. There was a chemist shop and a souvenir shop with bright coloured tropical clothes. He started to move out into the lobby when he spotted his aunt. She had her head down writing something. She was on the reception desk. Now he knew where she worked, he would avoid this area.

He walked back outside and followed the line of the buildings until he came to see the line of the sea. Turning to his left, he explored the bar area and saw the outdoor restaurant with its high pillars and open sides, shaded by the high roof. If he had walked through the lobby to this end, he would have found the swimming pool. He looked at this long glinting pool now. Children were splashing about and young women were lounging on the deck chairs trying not to get their swimsuits wet.

Chad breathed in this scene. This was more like it! He strolled down to the beach and took off his sneakers. He waded into the clear warm water. Tiny fishes darted away on both sides. The sky had two or three small cream puffs of cloud, but the blue surrounded him and he closed his eyes putting his face to the warmth of the sun.

Later in the morning he went swimming in his shorts and dried out on a deck chair. He knew enough not to spend too much time in this sun, he didn't want to ruin any more days by being burnt as well as bruised!

Lunchtime came and he watched as groups of people went into the restaurant. They were choosing from a long buffet, crammed with every sort of delicious food. He was getting hungry. But, it was still too early to be sent home, so he put aside the thought of appearing to his aunt. He fell to thinking of how he could sneak some of the food.

He noticed that some people just wandered in and sat with their family or friends. They walked straight past the waitress at the entranceway. If they looked like they knew where they were going, she took no notice of them. He wondered if he could just try.

He put his T-shirt on and his sneakers and tried to look casual. He waited until a family with two children close to his age entered, and then he followed as close as he could. He went up the three steps to the restaurant. Glancing quickly at the waitress, he could see that she was taking no notice of him.

He turned from following the group and mingled with the diners selecting their lunches. He knew he couldn't go and sit at a table. It would be too obvious. He couldn't take a plate, so he looked at all the mouth-watering dishes and decided that the best he could do was to pick up a bun, put some ham and cheese into it and as secretly as possible, put this into his pocket. He would take a few grapes too.

No one noticed an eleven-year old boy hungrily evaluating the food. No one noticed when he couldn't resist eating a little chocolate cake, right as he stood by the desserts. No one noticed as he sauntered back out of the restaurant. He found a spot away from the hotel, under a palm tree and there he demolished as slowly as he could, the stolen bun.

He swam again in the afternoon and dried out once more, watching people enjoying their holidays in this paradise. He couldn't bring himself to think of the dark, close room and the scuttling in the night. Reluctantly, he decided it was time. He would have to own up and see his aunt. He made his way down the lobby toward the reception desk.

Aunt Sa was not there. He hurried out to the staff car park. The truck was gone! He had left it too late. He hadn't seen a phone at his uncle's house and Chad was now too scared to phone even if there was one. He would have to think. Maybe he could stay here and meet his aunt when she arrived the next morning? It was the only plan that came to mind right at that moment.

To take his mind off his plight, he wandered in the afternoon down to the neighbouring hotel. It was older and the architecture was more traditional. It had dark beams of wood and cabinets with ancient artifacts of the Fijian people. He saw a display of pictures of ancient Fijian hairdos. He had seen people at home with hairdos like that. They weren't so new after all.

This hotel made him feel lonely and a bit afraid. It was too somber. He went back to his aunt's hotel. It was more modern and was painted in light and clean colours. The evening came quickly and he was starting to feel hungry again. He didn't think he would get away with his lunch time trick. People were more formal going to dinner. He thought he had better find somewhere to hide for the night. Maybe he could sleep in a cupboard?

With his tummy rumbling, he wandered down the corridors. He noticed that outside some doors people had put trays with discarded dinner plates. On one he found a banana. On another he found an orange and then the best of all was a plate where there was a whole small pizza totally untouched. He checked that the corridor was clear and he lifted the plate and ran outside to find some dark place to devour his dinner.

This would not be so bad. He began to think he could live here for the two weeks and then just appear on the last day, for his uncle to take him to the airport. He could put up with any lecture or thumping if it was that far away. It was his only option. He had proved he could survive. He had been careful to find a tap to give him drinking water all day and now he had found a way to provide himself with meals.

Since his aunt had gone, he found the best place now was in the lobby, right by the reception desk. There were long comfortable couches and if the staff closed up for the night, this was to be the place he would sleep. He sat watching people come and go from the desk. It was getting late but they still had staff working. He worried that soon someone might ask where his family was. He was just starting to think about finding somewhere else for the rest of the night, when a mini bus stopped at the entrance and another group of holidaymakers spilled out into the lobby.

Amongst the group was a young couple with a girl who looked too old to be their daughter. The man and woman were ignoring the girl as she trailed behind them up to the desk. She put her bag down and did a circuit of her surroundings with her gaze.

Chad's eyes widened. It had to be! It couldn't be anyone else! And she had said she was coming to Fiji as well. It was India! She looked taller than in her pictures and somehow prettier. She was wearing a sundress and her dark hair was tied in a bushy ponytail. Seeing her gave him a funny feeling, like seeing a film star in the flesh.

He wanted to hide. The couple would find out who he was and send him back to his uncle. He got up and walked as nonchalantly as he could to the shops. Here he turned and watched as the group checked in. India was walking about smiling and admiring the palm trees growing right in the middle of this wide covered alley of a lobby. Chad was willing her to come his way but she strayed further and further up toward the pool. Gradually she turned and re-met with the couple. The woman handed her something and pointed almost directly at Chad. A chill went through him, then he realised that she was pointing at the corridor behind him. He had moved behind a pillar just in case.

The man and women walked right past Chad, and he watched as India walked down toward the pool. He moved out from the pillar and followed her. She was already kneeling to test the temperature, sending ripples across the tranquil dark water. He had a horrible thought that maybe he had been mistaken, but just then India turned.

Chad moved a few steps closer and India stood straight and looked at him quizzically.

"Are you here on holiday?"

"Uh, yeah. Holiday. I'm on holiday." Chad admitted stupidly.

"Me too. I love this place!" There was no doubt about it. Chad had heard her voice on Skype, through his computer.

"India!"

The girl froze then moved a little closer. "Chad!" Her face lit with a grin. "You didn't tell me you were staying here!"

"Well, I'm not. Not really!"

"But you're here!"

"It's a long story."

"Try me."

Chad and India went over to the deck chairs and sat in the warm tropical evening air. Chad's story spilled out about his uncle and the escape. After he had finished his tale, they both sat and tried to think of what he should do.

"I can't believe we have met up, right here!" India shook her head at the astonishing turn of destiny. "It must be meant to be."

India said that Chad couldn't stay outside all night. Someone would get suspicious sooner or later. She had her own room and he could sleep on the floor. She had her key and they went to find where the room was. It was next to Sharon's but when they went in, they were pleased to find two beds. Chad gratefully curled into this comfortable bed, in the air-conditioned room. He could hear no scuttling and expected no roosters but he could still hear the chirping noise. He didn't care. He fell asleep almost at once.

Chapter Four
HIDING OUT

The two woke early and began to whisper. There was no sound of movement from Sharon's room yet. Chad had a warm shower and borrowed a clean T-shirt from India. It fit quite well and was just a plain white.

"You might even fit some of my shorts."

"I'm not wearing any of your undies!" He protested. He'd rather wear none and wash the ones he had worn the day before since India was complaining about him wearing undies for two days in a row. They would dry out pretty quick. Chad couldn't really see what the fuss was all about. She was starting to sound like his mother.

"Let's get out of here before Sharon comes. I don't think I could explain this!"

Just as India said this there was a knock at the door. "Daisy? Are you up?"

"Quick! Go out into the garden!" Fortunately the room was on the ground floor; Chad hurried out the open door onto the little patio and gathered up the wet T-shirt and undies that had been hanging on the outdoor chair. He walked just a safe distance from the room. He could see India talking to Sharon in the doorway. She was nodding. In a few minutes the coast was clear and Chad returned. He draped the clothes back on the chair.

"It's ok. We can talk now." India said. "They've gone to breakfast. I said I'd go later. Sharon wanted to know how come I'd used both beds. I had to say I had found one too hard and so I'd moved."

"Breakfast. That would be good."
"I've thought of that. It will be easy. Sharon said you just give the room number and they put it all on one bill at the end. Dad's paying. He won't notice. We'll go down later and I'll just give this room number for both of us."
"Do you think I should see my aunt today?"
India pulled a sour face. "It would be awful going back to your uncle's right now. Why don't you hide again today and see her tomorrow? It's going to be more fun if we can have some holiday together. I thought I'd be bored on my own and now here you are! It's meant to be."
Chad was easily convinced. The memory of his uncle's house was getting darker and darker and there was no way he wanted to trade this luxury for the dirt and weeds of the garden. Besides, he wanted to delay the punishment that would surely come. The thought of Gordon's menacing eye made him shudder.
"We should go for a walk incase they come back," suggested India.
They walked to the beach and Chad felt a little shy. He didn't really know India; she had just been like a computer character up until last night. Now he wasn't sure what to say. He hadn't had any girls as friends before either and he didn't know what girls talked about.
"Tell me about your mum." She demanded. "Is she pretty? Is she kind? Does she nag you all the time? Have you got any brothers or sisters?"
"She's nice. She's the best mum I know. I think she's still pretty. But she's old though."
"How old?"
"I think she's at least thirty."

"Dad's in his thirty's too. Did I tell you he has a stink girlfriend now?"

"Yeah."

"What about your mum? Does she have anyone? You said you lived with her on your own."

"She used to. We had another dad for about five years, Mike's dad. My dad left when I was a baby. Mikey's dad came along when I was about two, I think. Mum says she was on the rebound, whatever that means. He was mean to mum. He never worked. He just sat around the house eating and watching sport. Then he left us. I was pretty hurt at the time because I thought he was my real dad."

"Have you ever met your real dad?"

"No. All I know is he lives in Australia. Mum never talks about him."

"Haven't you even seen photos?"

"No she's locked them all away. She used to get angry when I asked too many questions. I get the feeling he really hurt her. I've seen her looking at the photos in her room sometimes and she always has a funny sort of look on her face, like she's wishing it were different. I think she never wanted him to go."

"My dad doesn't talk much about my mother either. He's got pictures. I carry one with me because it is all I know of my mum. I wish I could've known her, she has a lovely face. She was a beauty queen I think or something like that. She must've been because she must have had someone else fall in love with her. I think dad was very hurt too, he never uses her name. Just says 'your mother', if he ever talks does about her. I wish I could see her, even just once. I am sure she must think of me. I don't think a mother with that face would've wanted to lose me. And, I wish I had a mum, like my friends do."

"Why can't parents just stay with their kids? It isn't fair!" Chad wanted to end this conversation. At least India had a dad who was rich and who cared about her. All he knew of his own dad was what his uncle had told him. His own dad was a lazy slob. He probably had a fat gut and hairs coming out of his big floppy ears.

"Let's go to breakfast." He said.

"I s'ppose it will be ok now," agreed India. On the way, India turned back. "I'm just going to go back and get the photo of my mum. I want you to see it." I'll show you while we have breakfast.

Chad shrugged. He was more interested in the food.

He waited for India and then together they went into the restaurant. It went just as India had said. This time he could sit down at a table, go back for as much food as he wanted and he could have bacon and eggs and pancakes and juice. The pancakes weren't as good as Sa's but they were pretty good.

Chapter Five
THE BIG SECRET

When they had eaten, India pulled a photo from her skirt pocket. It was quite small. She laid it in front of Chad. He felt sick. It had nothing to do with the amount of pancakes he had just eaten. He knew this photo! It was his own mother when she was twenty-one! She had the same photo at home. He had often seen this photo!

"That's not your mother!" He finally got out.

"It is! It is! Dad has lots of photos of her; photos with him and her, wedding photos. This one's my favourite and is small enough for me to carry everywhere I go."

"NO! This can't be *your* mother! This is *my* mother!"

"No." India blinked. "What are you saying Chad? This is your mother? You must be getting her mixed up. She must look like your mother."

"No. Mum has exactly the same photo. This is a photo from when she was 21."

"Yes, her 21st birthday, when dad proposed to her."

"I didn't know that!"

"Well, he did. I wish I could show you the other photos. It would prove it to you that this is my mother!"

"That means…."

They both sat with startled faces, eyes wide with shock.

"That I'm your sister!"

For a long few minutes the two just stared at each other.

"I can see it!" India broke the silence. "You look like a miniature of dad. You even have the same hair! Same eye colour, same sort of way you both blink slowly. Your face is a bit different in shape but I can't believe I haven't noticed this before!"

"You don't look so much like mum, but you do have her coloured hair. Her hair is just a bit curly...."

"Can't you see! This is meant to be!"

Chad was still trying to get used to the thought that he had a sister. How on earth had this come about? Why didn't he know about a sister? Then in his mind he recalled his uncle saying "Didn't think he knew about *her*". He had assumed Gordon was talking about the women his father must have run off with. Now he realised he was talking about India. India. That wasn't even her real name.

"What is your real name anyway?"

"Eileen."

"My mother's name! That's why your dad prefers to call you Daisy!"

Both suddenly wanted to know all about their parents. Chad began to get a picture of a man who was anything but lazy. He was a big property developer on the Gold Coast. He made a lot of money and India was always moving from one wonderful apartment to a better one. India discovered a mother who doted on her children and that she also had another half brother, Mike. This made them both sad. Why couldn't their parents just get on so that they could all be together?

34

Chad then realized, that he had met India because she had added him from her aunt's page. He had been checking to add to her friend list, and as she had been looking at peoples home pages, she had spotted her apartment in the picture that Chad had taken on his holiday.

So, now there were more family members to explain to Chad. He had two aunts who lived in Queensland, his father's sisters. Chad had never even heard of them. Brother and sister were still crazy to know more about what had happened, and why their family could not have stayed together. It seemed so unfair. India almost used her favourite saying again to exclaim that finding each other must have been 'meant to be'.

"Sharon knows more about what happened. She finds out everything. I'm going to see what she knows." India decided. "I think she knows more than she's told me."

The day was wonderful and strange. Chad had never had a sister before and India had never had a brother. They kept saying things like, "I do that too!" or, "Dad loves eating hot spicy food as well." Lunchtime was another feast. Sharon and her boyfriend were seen only once in the distance trying to get a hobby cat to glide across the bay. "Sharon will just think I've befriended someone. She'll be glad she doesn't have to have me with her all day long," said India.

For Chad's sake, they went to dinner early so that he could eat. India decided to go back and have her meal later so that she could quiz Sharon. She would join her and her boyfriend for dinner and try to get her talking.

India knew that if she waited until the wine had mellowed Sharon, she would say more than she should. She had to wait until she could talk to Sharon alone.

"Can I go for a walk to the beach with you? Just you and me, I mean." She pleaded.

Sharon looked to her boyfriend. He reluctantly nodded. "I'll be in the bar." He said and wandered off. India and Sharon walked down toward the beach by the light of the outdoor lamps. They sat on the wall looking out at the stars and the reflection of the moon as it broke into wavy lines with each little push of the water to the shore.

"Can I ask you something?" India probed.

"I knew something was coming." Sharon laughed. "Go on ask me."

"What do you know about how I ended up with dad? Most kids end up with their mums when relationships break up. How come I ended up with dad?"

"Oh... I don't think I can go there. One day your dad might tell you more. I think he's a bit embarrassed about the whole thing, the whole mess." She threw her hand to her mouth. "I don't mean it was a mess that you were with him! I mean. Well, it was sort of a mess, but I know he loves you. He's never regretted what he did."

"Why would he regret what he did? What did he do that he would regret? Keeping me? Was that the mess? Am I just a pest to dad?" She faked a look of self-pity. She knew this would draw more out from Sharon.

"No! You're not a pest. He just made a big mess when he ran off with you."

"Ran off with me? Didn't mum agree to him having me?"

"You're not supposed to know all this."

"You know it! It is my life! I promise I'll never tell dad that you told me. Please I want to know!"

"He doesn't know I know."

"Just tell me Sharon. I have a right to know!"

"When you were little, your mum and dad split up. Your mum had another baby, a boy I think, and you were only about two. They argued about who was going to keep you children and your dad could see that the courts would always favour the mother. He couldn't bear to leave both of you, but he couldn't see how he could take your brother since he was still being breast-fed. He decided that he was going to keep you at least. So he took off. Went to Australia and basically kidnapped you."

"That's pretty bad eh? My mother must have tried to find me?"

"She did try but as you know, your dad is pretty clever. He was undetected until you were old enough to go to school.   Then he was in a dilemma, schools asked questions and he was under a lot of pressure."

"So it all came out. So she found me. But I am still with dad?"

"No. Your dad in the meantime went all religious. He got a guilty conscience I think. His business partner, Ted told me that. Ted thinks that this is why your dad is such a churchgoer. He'd had enough hell already!" She chuckled. "Anyway, after he had this big change of heart, he went to the police and coughed up. Then it was all on. They were going to charge him. The New

Zealand law got involved. It was a big fight. Your mother was hysterical. She was now with someone else and had another child."

"Mikey" India muttered.

"Eh?"

"Nothing.......... Crikey!... I said..."

"Your dad was already well on his way to getting wealthy and he employed the best lawyers. In the end your mum took a payout and dropped charges. She must be a money grubber, you're better off with your dad I reckon, even if he did steal you in the first place."

"So dad got custody of me."

"Yep. That's about it. Don't you ever let on that I told you anything!" Sharon tried to look intimidating. India ignored the look. So this was the truth.

When she and Chad went out later to walk and talk it through, Chad was infuriated. "Money grubber! My mother's so poor, she has to work two jobs to feed us and pay for the things Mike needs. She would have had to think about getting you back or getting specialist treatment for Mike. Since we still had Mike's dad with us at the time, I guess he wouldn't have wanted another mouth to feed. Not that he ever earned anything! She must have thought you were getting a better life, just where you were. Now I know why she is always so sad."

"Oh, love to hear that she is sad.... Because she misses me! Oh, not because she is sad. Oh, it is all so terrible! Do you think mum could ever love dad again? He's different from when they were married. I think dad has never stopped loving mum."

38

"I don't know. It is a dream. We'll never know."

"I don't know about that…" India's eyes narrowed and a sly smile twisted her mouth.

"What are you thinking?"

"What if we both disappeared? I'll bet your uncle's pretty worried about where you are right now, but what if we both disappeared for days? Our parents would have to come to Fiji to try to find us! We could make them meet up somehow!"

"Yeah, then they could just kill each other!"

"No! Don't you see? It's meant to be!"

"Meant to be, yeah…." Chad wasn't so sure.

"What we are going to do is run away to one of those little islands. We can eat coconuts and any fruit we find on the island."

Now Chad became more interested. "How will we get there? I don't think we can go by hobby cat."

"Of course not! But didn't you see? There are some little dinghies that they take down in the morning.   People hire them.   We can get one of those."

"With what? They cost heaps!"

"Dad gave me heaps! I've got plenty to spend. The boats might be thirty, that's nothing! We need to plan. I can get them to hire me a boat; I'm told I look older than I am."

"How will we get our parents to meet up?"

"We'll think about that. We need to fill my beach-bag with extra clothes and see if we can get a knife from the dining room to cut into fruit or whatever we might need a knife for. Tomorrow at breakfast, we'll get a knife. I'll take my beach-bag and we'll try to get some food wrapped in tissues to take as well, just incase it takes a few hours to get to an island. I will take the glasses from the room too, so we can drink water from the island waterfall"

India had read too many fantasy books and thought that every island would have a crystal pool with a waterfall. It would be obvious. Even on TV, people who were lost on islands could find a waterfall and plenty of coconuts to eat. It seemed like a fun thing to do.

Chad could hardly sleep even though the bed was comfortable. He was excited about the plan. He kept trying to think of how to get their parents to meet. He thought about how he had met India on the net. Of all the millions of people in the world, he met his own sister. He was starting to think, 'it's meant to be'.

Chapter Six
AT SEA

Just as Chad woke he had it! He had the way they could get their parents to meet.

"What we'll do is see if we can send a message from the hotel by email. You send one to your dad, telling him to meet you at the restaurant in two days time at seven PM. By then he'll know you've gone missing. I'll send a message to my mother the same!"

"What a great idea! I'll have to do this because you can't go near the office. All you have to do is give me your mum's email address."

First they made the second bed in case Sharon looked into the room and then went to breakfast. Chad looked longingly at the buffet and wondered what he would get to eat in the following days.

They managed to fill half the beach bag with buns, fruit and four miniature packets of rice bubbles. Chad stole a knife from the table and two spoons. India went to the hotel shop and bought four bottles of drink. The bag was repacked to put extra clothes in the bottom and the glasses from the room.

Chad's dry undies and T-shirt went in and enough extra T-shirts and shorts that they could both wear. India had already bought Chad a toothbrush, and she remembered to pack suncream and two hats. Chad could wear her cap. She only had one pair of sunglasses. "We'll take some soap too; we will wash in the pool with the waterfall."

India was a great actress. She had no problem getting the office to let her send two emails. They let her send them by herself and said they would put the charge for the service on to her room bill.

"No problem," said India.

As India left the office she noticed a small article on the front of the Fiji Times. The heading read:

"Boy from New Zealand missing in Fiji"

She took a copy of the paper and ran to where Chad was waiting in the garden. They sat outside the hotel room on the outdoor chair and India read the article.

"Chad Linders came to Fiji on holiday on Friday but ran away from his Uncle Gordon Maine's home on Monday. Although his uncle has searched around the area and in Nadi, no sign has been seen of Chad. "The boy is not a very stable boy. He suffers from delusions" His uncle stated. "He was having such a wonderful holiday and we had been to the beach and I had thought he was so happy, but now he has done this and I am so worried. His mother is begging me to find him. He is an uncaring boy to worry his mother like this."" Mr Maine is asking for people to look out for Chad. He is eleven years old and has blond curly hair. He was last seen wearing blue shorts and a white T-shirt with a picture of himself, holding a white rat, imprinted on it. He was wearing black and white sneakers. If anyone knows his whereabouts, please contact the Nadi police station.'

Chad was glad that right now, he was now wearing India's T-shirt and had bare feet. He looked up at the hotel buildings all around him and felt very exposed. Suppose someone was looking out of one of the windows and recognised him as an eleven-year-old, curly headed, blond boy? They had to get away as fast as possible. He jammed India's cap onto his head and tried to cover has much of his hair as possible.

It was noon before they saw the Fijian water-sports man bringing down the run about dinghies. They decided to risk lunch as a last meal before going out as Chad was hungry again. No one looked at them with anything other than bored interest. By the time they got down to the beach they couldn't see the sports equipment man.

India had her money in a purse in her hand ready to find out how much it might be for hire. They waited for a long time but no one came along. One of the boats sat in the water with the outboard motor tipped, ready for someone to use.

"Let's just take it," said India. "We aren't planning to bring it back today anyway."

"That's stealing!" Chad was horrified.

"So is not bringing it back!"

"I guess so."

India was tugging Chad to the little boat. "Come on help me push it into the water, its heavy."

Chad and India pushed the boat onto the waves. It bounced a little as they pushed it past the first few footsteps. "Get in!" India commanded. Chad climbed aboard. India pushed it a little further and then joined him in the boat. "Can you start one of these things?"

"Of course! Dad taught me! I mean my other dad, Mike's dad."

Chad had to try a couple of times to get the motor running but soon it was chugging and smoking and he turned the boat and steered it out to sea. He watched the shore with worry, looking for the sport's man to come out and chase them in another boat. No one followed. Gradually the buildings became smaller and more distant. They just steered in a straight line away from the beach. The waves became a bit bigger and they motored over them, being splashed with water as it fought against their progress.

It was cooler out at sea but they both covered themselves with sunblock and wore their hats. They had been trained well. Chad was already getting quite brown and his nose had a little too much pink already.

After an hour of motoring they couldn't see the resort any longer. The big main island's coast was always to their right but now they could see small islands, some just a hump in the water with white sand and a little green hat on top. They would need something a little bigger than this to hide on; they needed one with coconut trees for food too.

It was the hottest part of the day and as they travelled, more and more islands came into view. Some looked to have big buildings on them and they didn't want to go there, they would be caught before they had laid their plot for their parents. They had been going along like this for some time when the motor on the outboard began to cough and splutter.

Finally the motor died.

"What do we do now?" Chad asked.

"Row."

"With what?"

They hunted about feeling more and more panicked, but there were no oars. There was nothing in the little boat, not even an anchor.

Chapter Seven
TREASURE

The dark came quickly in the tropics. Though it was still warm and the moon was still giving a lot of light, this was no help. They were drifting aimlessly in the boat. The islands around them hadn't changed much but some were a little closer than they had been before. Neither of them wanted to think about sharks.

They had rationed the drinks and one bottle each had been emptied and a little of the second bottle. They had eaten the squashed buns and some of the fruit and all of the rice bubbles. Chad had eaten three boxes. It was starting to feel cool. Out at sea it could get cooler still and the clouds were starting to build in the sky, covering the lights of the stars.

They watched in horror as the moon disappeared and they could see nothing around them. Just the lapping of the waves and a splot of rain falling on the water and into their boat broke the quiet. It was an uneasy quiet. Night dragged on as they rocked. There was nothing to say. Both were regretting the idea that had seemed so good to begin with. Their parents were going to come up to Fiji just to find them drowned.

They sat together, India comforting Chad with her arm around him. They felt a bit warmer sitting close and trying to see anything in the dark. The rain hadn't been for long but they were both now wet and cold. They were afraid the boat might be well out to sea by now. Chad didn't know when it happened, but he fell asleep.

He was woken suddenly with a jolt. India must have been asleep too because she lurched forward and both lost balance.

"Ouch!" She said as she bumped her arm on the side of the boat.

"What was that?" Chad asked nervously. He could imagine a sea monster or a whale under the boat. A crunching sound and another lurch of the boat made them realise they had beached.

"Land! Quick let's get out and drag the boat up. I hope this island has coconut trees!"

India was back in control and feeling much happier.

"I don't care if it has or not. I just want to get off this boat. I'd go back to Uncle Gordon's rather than sit in this death trap all night!"

Chad jumped off the side of the boat onto soft sand and tropical warm water up to his knees. He clutched the side of the boat and held it steady for India to get out. Then the two of them dragged the boat up on to the sand. They tried to make out what the island looked like. Maybe they were back on the mainland?

As they made their way up the shoreline, India remembered her beach bag. She went back and got it from the boat and slung it over her shoulder. The bottles clinked inside.

"Well, we could always send a message in a bottle. I've heard of that, but we haven't got any paper or pen!" Chad reminded anxiously.

They climbed up over some small black rocks that were covered in weedy low growing vines. Once up on the land they saw a little hut. There were no lights on but beyond it was a path and on it was a small light to show the pathway. They walked around the hut and in the light of the little lamp they could see that it was a resort hut, a 'bure'.

They went back around to the beach side of the building and stepped on to the balcony. The blinds were closed across the French doors, but there was a gap between them. India peered into the darkness of the bure.

"It looks empty." She whispered.

"How can you be sure?"

"It doesn't look like there is any bedding on the beds."

She tried the door and it gave. It slid with a noisy grinding sound as she pulled it open.

"Shhh" She admonished herself.

They crept in half expecting someone to challenge them any minute.

"Don't turn any lights on!" India whispered loudly as she saw Chad reach for the switch.

As India had said, there was no one staylng in this room. There was a bare mattress on a double bed and a bare mattress on a single bed. Pillows and blankets were stored in a cupboard above the wardrobe. They gratefully pulled these down and settled for the rest of the night. As the night went on a wind grew and rain began in earnest splashing and beating against the little bure.

Chad couldn't believe it. Even here there was a chirping noise in the room. His last thought as he fell asleep was, 'What made that noise?'

India shook Chad awake. The sun was up but it was a dull cloud covered day. The rain had stopped but the clouds were bunched in dark pillows, heavy in the sky. The sea had stirred and was covered in whitecaps that rolled in breakers on the sand beneath the bure. India went to the window and with horror, realised that their boat was gone! Even if they had wanted to use it again, there was now no chance; the sea had claimed it in the night.

There was nothing for it but to explore this island. Chad went into the bathroom and showered. India noticed that some of the tiles were broken and some had been removed.

"I think I know why no one's staying in this room. They're fixing it." She concluded. "We had better put everything back during the day. We can come here safely at night but someone might work in it during the day. We'll hide my beach bag under the deck."

"I don't like to bring it up India…. But.."

"You're hungry. I know. I could've guessed. Let's go see what we can find."

They walked along the path. In the distance they could see a collection of low built buildings in a group. "Looks like the dining room to me." Said Chad.

They could see now that their bure was the last one at the end of the island. It was furthermost from all the main parts of this little island resort. The whole island was tiny; they guessed that they could walk right around it in about ten minutes. At the front there was a signpost that read, TREASURE ISLAND.

Many of the other rooms must have been full. There were again groups of people and couples making their way to breakfast. The smell of the bacon cooking was drawing Chad like a cat to the fridge.

"We don't know what the system is here." India said. "But if my experience of hotels is anything, I think we'll be able to pay for something in cash. I still have nearly $100. I think we will be able to live quite well here for a few days."

They ordered just toast much to Chad's annoyance. The breakfast buffet looked better but India was the authority and it was her money. "We have to be careful. If breakfast takes a quarter of our money then how will we pay for dinner?"

They spent the day exploring and swimming and discovering so many beautiful bright coloured fish and corals that they had never imagined would be just so close to the island. A staff member called Josiah told them that this was a marine reserve. No one was allowed to damage or take the coral. They learned that coral is a living creature. A colony of coral could be one hundred or maybe even one thousand years in the making. Watching the dance of the bright coloured fishes in a magical sea garden was hard to leave.

Close by they could see another small island about the same size as the one they were already on. It had one big wooden building and later in the morning they saw a lovely old sailing boat moor at this island. Their new friend Josiah told them that this was Beachcomber Island where lots of young people go and stay in dormitories. He grinned as he told them of the parties and the music and the university students who would come up in groups from Australia and New Zealand, to have fun all night.

No kids were allowed to stay on Beachcomber Island, but in the day big groups of day trippers came and had lunch on the island, before sailing back in the afternoon on the Tui Tai, the boat they were admiring. Day-trippers stayed for the buffet lunch, it was all included in their ticket.

If the two wanted to go over to Beachcomber for a look it was easy. They could go over on one of the little glass bottom boats that travelled back and forth during the day. This idea appealed to Chad. It appealed to India too, who was trying to think of ways to feed her bottomless pit of a brother.

"Don't you see? If we go across when the Tui Tai is in, we can blend in with the day-trippers and have lunch free! No one will notice a couple of extra kids."

It worked. Lunch was a feast. After they had eaten and had beached themselves on the wide coral sand apron, in front of the main building, they returned to their 'own' island.

"I don't know if we could get away with that twice. Maybe if we tried to look different somehow we could do this the day after tomorrow."

"We can always eat coconuts" Said Chad, a bit rueful that they hadn't been able to try surviving alone on an uninhabited island. That led to a fruitless afternoon where Chad tried for hours to break into a coconut fresh from the tree. No matter how hard he hacked at the husk he couldn't part it. Josiah laughed and laughed, then made it look like it was the peel of a banana as he husked the big nut on a sharp stick.

He delighted the two by climbing a coconut tree, clinging with his feet as he ascended. He threw down two more nuts and cut them with a machete so that they could drink the sweet fresh milk inside. Chad loved the soft fresh flesh and used his spoon from the hotel he had stolen before they left in the boat, to scoop as much as he could.

Josiah left them with a warning. "You have to be careful with Mr Coconut tree. He likes to throw his coconuts at little boys who steal from him. The coconut will try to be careful because he has eyes. But people get killed by Mr Coconut tree." He winked as he told Chad this.

"Do you think it's true?" He asked India.

"I wouldn't want to be clonked on the head with one." She scowled. "I'm going to the girl's room." She stated and Chad was left to wander about on his own.

He walked about looking out for trees with coconuts that might be ready to drop. He was starting to go off thinking coconuts were so desirable. Perhaps this was why he was looking up and almost didn't see the man coming straight toward him. Almost too late he looked and was only feet from Baldy! Chad quickly turned on his heels and hurried for somewhere to hide.

He was shaking with fear as he peered from behind the wall of the games room. There was no doubt about it. It was Baldy! What was he doing on Treasure Island? Surely his uncle hadn't sent him out here to look for his nephew and how would he know to come to this very island?

Chad ran to find India. She was found talking to Josiah. She waved goodbye to Josiah and met Chad.

India said. "I had to try to find some way not to lie, but Josiah kept asking me which couple was my parents. I had to say I hadn't seen them most of the day. They could be asleep. That's true isn't it? What's wrong with you? You look like you've seen a monster!"

"Sort of... No worse! It's Baldy!"

"Who?"

"Remember I told you Uncle Gordon went off to drink kava with a Fijian man and Baldy? Well, I've just seen him." Chad was trying to catch his nervous breathe, "And what is weirder is, now I remember where I have seen him before! He was in one of your pictures. In the one with the new apartment you have moved too. He was sitting in the café at the bottom. I am sure it's the same man!"

"Which one, show me the man."

They hid by a wall and looked into the bar. India studied this man carefully.

"I've seen his face too. I'm not sure why but he looks familiar. Like I've seen him on the news or something"

"I don't like him and I don't trust him," said Chad.

They were not happy when they realised that Baldy was staying in the bure right next to their bure. He went out snorkelling in the afternoon, his bald head was going red from the sun and he came back cursing and touching the sore spots on his head. For the rest of the afternoon he was all on his own in his room and he kept his curtains drawn. Chad and India watched as the day wore on and in the dusk a small boat came to the shore and Baldy met it.

There was another man on board but Chad and India couldn't make out who it was. The two rowed out in the boat. In between the two men was a big metal box. For about an hour, the boat bobbed as a silhouette against the now clear sky. There were lights flickering in and out of the boat. Then the boat returned Baldy to the shore. The second man left with the box. The boat was riding low in the water and further out the boat connected with a bigger boat and was gone.

Baldy was singing softly to himself. Soon he went off to the bar and the singing became louder and ruder and Chad and India stopped spying on him. They returned to their bure. As much as they wanted to look in Baldy's bure, they were not so sure he wouldn't catch them.

.

Chapter Eight
THE MEETING

Chad's mother Eileen was still teary as she sat down at the table in the restaurant. Gordon was patting her hand.

"It'll be OK. I'll discipline the little terror when I catch him."

"Please Gordon, leave this to me. I just can't imagine what has gotten into his head."

"You drove him away Gordon." Sa said quietly but firmly. "Poor little boy. He was made to be a slave. I have to tell Eileen the truth. It was you Gordon. I'm not afraid of you anymore; I have to tell the truth."

Chad's mother looked at Gordon with anger. "I should never have believed you. You said you would give Chad a great holiday. I'll bet he never saw anything but the inside of his room! He hates to be cooped up."

"Don't you stick your beak in Sa! I'll deal with you later. Cooped up! He had plenty outdoor fun! I know what boys like to do on holiday! What do you think I am? He's my nephew, as close to me as my own elbow."

But Eileen wasn't listening. She sucked in her breath. She was staring at the entrance to the restaurant. "I don't believe it! What is *HE* doing here?"

A tall athletic man walked in to the restaurant. He was alone and looking about with concern all over his face, searching everyone in the room. His eyes came to rest on Eileen and he stopped, he looked pale, but nodded to himself.

Before she could run, Mark was at her table.

"Hello Eileen."

"Hello Mark."

"Gordon...." Said Mark.

"Yes. It's me Mark and we are in the middle of some family business," snarled Gordon as he rose as if to push Mark away from the table.

Eileen snapped out of her shock. "No... Gordon..."

"I think I can give some answers to some of that 'family business'," said Mark quietly.

"Then you had better start talking!" Gordon moved forward and grabbed Mark's shirt collar. "You been kidnapping again! I'll kill you!"

"Sit down!" Screamed Eileen and Sa at the same time. "Let Mark talk."

Mark shook his head then laughed a feeble a laugh. "It's meant to be.."

"You might laugh but we are worried off our brains here! Chad's missing!" Growled Gordon. Adding, "Yes, your son Chad! Does that worry you or do you know about this some how. This is your doing isn't it?"

"No. Quite wrong Gordon. Other forces have been at work here, and other small minds. You see, Daisy.. I mean Eileen is missing too..."

Eileen sucked air in a gasp. "My baby!" She started to cry.

"They've met each other, they know about each other." Mark said simply. "This is their plan. I just know they will be ok."

"Didn't I say it?" Grumbled Gordon. "Come out in the wash. It always does."

Eileen sniffed but stopped crying.

Aunt Sa stood up. "Gordon it's time for us to go. We're going to the bar!"

"But you don't drink! I don't want to go to the bar right now! I give the orders!"

"Gordon. *You* need a drink." Sa said firmly.

He moved off huffing and growling and looking back with threatening glares toward Mark. Eileen watched them go as Mark took a seat.

"What is this all about Mark. You're the last person I ever wanted to see again."

"Really......?" He asked softly.

She didn't answer.

"When I received the email," Mark began 'meet me at this resort.' I thought Daisy was just bored and ignored it. Then when Sharon phoned and the police contacted me, I realised something was very odd. Dai.. Eileen is growing up. I don't have as much time to spend with her these days and I felt like I hardly knew what was going on in her life anymore. The thought of her disappearing sent me into terror.

The police asked me all sorts of questions about her activities and friends. Do you know I couldn't answer most of them? It made me feel bad. The only thing I did know was that she loved to spend a lot of time on the net. Can you imagine the horror that pulled up in my mind?"

"Chad is on the net for hours too."

"Yes, and that is how they met. I am sure that this is what has happened. By a strange, once in a million, coincidence and a shared love for travel and rats of all things, Daisy made contact with Chad. I found some of their old messages.

They didn't know that they were brother and sister but I think they've found out now. Sharon told me that Daisy was asking a lot of questions. She'd seen her with a younger boy a couple of days ago. You see Sarai works here, Chad must've hidden in the truck that brought her to work and somehow have met Daisy."

"What do we do now?"

"We wait. They'll give us some sign about where they are. Probably hiding right here in the hotel somewhere!"

"Why?"

"They wanted us to meet. India's favourite movie is a story like this, Don't you see? The email message? I gather you received one as well."

Eileen nodded. "They don't understand. You can't just turn back the clock."

"There's something I must ask you. But maybe we need to spend a bit more time before I ask you."

"Just ask me Mark. You can't hurt me anymore than you already have."

"I know that! But can't you see that I've changed? I admit it. I was young, selfish and cruel to you and I am so sorry. I wish I could turn the clock back on that!"

"No one really changes."

"Have you?"

She laughed wryly. "What do you think? With losing my baby, bringing up two boys alone and one with such great needs. You think I haven't had to change?"

"I am so, so sorry." Mark said. "That's what I wanted to ask you. Can you forgive me? I can't change the hurt, but I want to say sorry."

Eileen started to sniff again. She managed to say in a tiny voice. "I... want to."

Mark leaned toward her and took her hand. "You don't know how much I have thought of you through the years Eileen. I know it's probably too late, but I want you to know that no one has ever meant as much to me as you have."

"Me too." She said weakly.

"Haven't you forgotten something!" The loud obtrusive voice broke into their world. "There are two kids out there, maybe washed up drowned somewhere. Someone's got to care!" Gordon cleared this throat and looked about to find somewhere to spit.

"Not here Gordon!" Said Sa.

Mark said. "Eileen isn't come back to your house tonight Gordon, I'm booking a room for her right here at the hotel. If the kids mean to contact us, this is where they will come to. Eileen needs to be right here. With me."

Gordon looked from one to the other. "Whole family is as mad as each other. I'm off! C'mon Sa, we're going back to the house."

"Mad family." Eileen smiled as she looked up at Mark. He was better looking now than ever. His clothes showed money. He always had a way with business. Maybe part of their problems had come because she had never believed this and fought him on every decision he made.

"I don't know about madness." Mark went on, "more like strong willed I would say. And that strong will has emerged in Daisy... I mean, Eileen, too."

"Just call her Daisy. I like it. I am so scared to see her Mark. Scared and very happy. I just know things will work out."

59

"That's what she would say. 'It's meant to be'. I guess we just sit and wait for their next move. We need to fill the police in with all we know as well."

Chapter Nine
BALDY

On the island, India and Chad tried to imagine what was happening. Chad didn't think his mother would even talk to his dad. India was sure their dad would do ok. She thought their mum would either run away, or go soft and that was her hope.

"I think run away." Said Chad.

"We'll see."

"What do we do now?"

"Tomorrow maybe we should go to the office and send a message to the resort. They will come and get us."

"What's that noise?"

"I told you. It is the lizards. They make that chirping noise. I like them. They are so cute and fun to watch."

"No. *That* noise!"

It was a sound as if something heavy was being dragged near their bure. They both went silent to listen.

"Let's go outside to see." India was whispering again.

They tiptoed to the door and opened it as quietly as they could. Next door they could see Baldy outside his bure. It was dark but the path lamp showed him in the shadows hauling something quite big up to the bure. He stopped and left whatever it was by the deck and went inside. A few minutes later they saw him heading for the bar.

As soon as it was safe they went to see what the large shape was. A large sack, dank and smelling and a bit fishy sat on the sand. Chad wanted to look inside.

"No let's leave it alone. It is probably just fish."

But Chad was already working at the rope that tied the opening. He pulled back the sack and India gave a little cry. It was a turtle shell.

"No, not a shell," Said Chad. "A giant turtle!"

"Josiah said that they come up to the beach to lay eggs at certain times of the year. What is Baldy doing with this poor thing?"

"No good, you can be sure!"

"Oh, we have to set it free. Poor turtle!" India had no thought but to free this sea creature. "Help me to drag the turtle to the shore. We are going to put it back in the water. I hope it goes somewhere else!"

They puffed and dragged the sack with the turtle on its back. When they reached the water they heaved until they could turn it over. With effort they pulled the sack from the sea creature and stood back waiting for it to go. After a long time, its head came out of the shell and then the flippers. It began to haul itself into the water, sensing freedom. It was taking forever to go. Chad and India were willing it to move; hardly daring to look back incase Baldy returned.

"I can't stand it; I'm going back to put his smelly sack on his balcony so he knows the turtle got away! You stay and watch to make sure she does." India turned back to the bure.

She dropped the sack on the balcony and went to jump back down onto the sand when a strong arm snapped out and grabbed her arm. She wrestled and cried out. The big man clamped his hand over her mouth and dragged her, kicking, back into his bure.

"What have you been up to? Stupid girl!" He hissed in a surly tone. It was the iciest voice India had ever heard. She bit his hand. He slapped her cheek and she started to cry.

On the beach Chad was happily watching the turtle gracefully swimming out beyond his sight when he heard a thump and the bang of a door. He ran up the beach toward Baldy's bure. Just then he heard a sharp yell from India and he would have rushed to her rescue but stopped suddenly.

"What will be the use if he gets us both?" He asked himself out-loud.

He stood frozen just by the balcony and stepped back a bit more into the shadows.

He could hear them talking.

"That was worth a lot of money to me little girl. I have a good mind to let you know how mad that makes me."

"My dad will be looking for me. You have to let me go."

"Your dad won't know what became of you will he? You might just disappear, presumed drowned." He liked this joke and laughed a horrible gurgle-like laugh deep in his throat.

"My dad will hunt you down. He's a powerful man. He would see you in prison if you harm me!" She was trying to sound brave, but every now and then a terrified catch of her breath made her speech stutter.

"Oh, and who is this powerful dad? The USA President?" He gurgled again.

"My dad develops property. He'd turn this place upside down until he found you."

"Would he?" He scratched his burned bald head that now had one big blister right on top, and cursed at the pain. "Property developer. If you tell me his name, I might let you go."

Outside, Chad was whispering, trying to will India to stop talking. "Don't tell him! Don't say any more!"

"Mark Linders"

"Mark Linders! Oh yes a very wealthy man. Thank you for that young lady, I think I have found a better turtle! He might pay dearly to have you back!"

"Mark Linders?" Muttered Chad. So my mother never married Mike's dad, she still goes by the name of Linders. I never knew that! There had to be time to work that one out later but right now he needed to be thinking hard. How could he best help India?

"Tonight." Baldy said coldly, "I was going to deliver a turtle, but I think the boys will be just as happy to take care of you. Just a little while and the boat will be here. You don't have to wait long. And just so you don't get any big ideas, I'll be right here with you until it does."

Chad was sweating. It was late in the night and the temperature was at its coolest but trickles ran down his back. He leaned against the wall. "I can't leave India. But what can I do?"

He couldn't see that there was any other choice. Baldy didn't know he existed; he had to go and raise the alarm. He ran to the resort office. A relaxed lady greeted him with a leisurely "bula!"

64

"You gotta help me!"

"Whoa! What's the problem?"

"I've got to use the phone! Please!"

"Well, we don't let children use the phone. You can get your parents and they can make a call if they want to."

"No you don't understand! My sister is being kidnapped by a really evil man! I have to stop him!"

She laughed with merriment. What imagination children had!

"Please! I have to ring a resort back on the main island!"

"Oh? How will that help you?"

"That's where our parents are!"

"Then who are you staying with here?"

"No one! Just us. We're not meant to be here! Please! Help me!"

"I don't understand. You might have to tell me a bit more I think." She was quite amused.

"Look, I don't have time. She'll be gone any minute! Please! Send Josiah to the end bure! He'll see. He can help. Baldy is too big. I can't rescue her!"

"Baldy? But Josiah is asleep, like you should be."

"Look, do you have a newspaper?"

"Yes! I can do that for you. That's an easy request." She got up and slowly walked into the kitchen. Chad followed her hopping from one foot to the other. He took the newspaper and searched through the pages. "Oh, no! Do you have any old newspapers from a day or two ago?"

She laughed but went to a cushion and lifted it up. There were a number of old papers under the cushion in a pile and Chad had to dig until he found one that had anything he was looking for. The paper from the day before had an article on page two:

"Two children still missing in Fiji.

Chad Linders has not been seen since Monday and the daughter of Gold Coast property, developer, Mark Linders is also still missing. It is believed that although the names are the same, the two incidents are not related. Police are asking for any information from anyone siting either of these children.'

Chad pointed at the article. "Me! That's me! And we are related and our parents are waiting to hear from us at the resort! Please make the call for me! I must get help for India!"

"Ok, ok! Calm down, let me read the story first." She put on glasses and carefully read the story. "Hmm. I do remember the boy is supposed to be blond. This is all a bit strange. Come on. We'll make the call."

It took forever for the woman to find the telephone number then she slowly dialled the numbers. Chad was almost screaming. First she had a conversation in Fijian and laughed and talked and then seemed to remember Chad.

Eventually Chad's mother was located. As soon as Chad heard her voice he nearly choked and had to swallow a few times before he could speak.

"Get India's Dad! He has to get the police! He has to help. Baldy has got her in his bure and he's going to kidnap her!"

"India! Who? What? I can't understand you? Where are you?" She was almost hysterical with confusion.

"Treasure Island. We're on Treasure Island! You have to get the police!. Tell Daisy's father to get here now!"

"Please. Just stay put; both of you! Now we know where you are, we will come first thing tomorrow. I so want to help you but we can't come tonight there won't be any boats."

"Please mum believe me! You need to get the police!"

"We can handle this now. We'll let them know you have been found."

"NO!" He screamed. "You have to help me save India!"

"India? What on earth are you talking about? You are in Fiji!"

"No! India! Daisy. A man has her prisoner in his room!"

"What! Why didn't you say so!"

"Just get the police here now, get a helicopter. Get India's dad!"

The woman staff member had more of an idea now. She put her arm about Chad's shoulder. "Can you show me what room your sister is in?"

"Yes, but get someone big!"

Josiah was woken. He remembered Chad and India. He said he would come. He came out half-asleep and the three walked to the end of the island. No matter how hard Chad tried to hurry them, they were still unconvinced that there was any real danger. This was a holiday resort in Fiji, not the back streets of some big and dangerous city.

They reached Baldy's bure and there were no lights. Josiah knocked on the door but there was no answer.

"He's asleep I think."

"No." Said Chad. "We should go around the back."

The two staff members followed him reluctantly. The French door on the bure was wide open and the curtains were pulled back. Chad rushed in to the room and turned on a light. There was evidence of a scuffle. One of India's sandals lay by the bed. Chad spotted some of her coils of hair on the floor. "The filthy, fat, dog! He's pulled her by the hair!" He yelled. "It's too late, they've taken her!"

Chad ran out on to the balcony and looked on to the beach. He saw a light flickering just off the shore. The big boat was still there.

"Quick! She'll be on the boat! We have to stop them!"

Josiah was fully awake now and he looked like he was starting to believe Chad's story. "What is this boat? I have seen it other nights just out there. In the day it is goes into Lautoka then comes back out for the night. It is called the 'protector'. I've been wondering why it comes here."

"They were getting turtles! But we freed the turtle and now they've got India!"

Josiah said. "We'll make sure she will be ok. In the mean time I think you might have some things to tell us about?"

Chad was defeated. What more could he do? He was in big trouble. It was his entire fault and now India would be murdered and thrown to the sharks.

Chapter Ten
ENDINGS

Josiah and the woman were so kind. They even tried to get him to eat some chips. He wasn't hungry for the first time since he had been in Fiji. He couldn't sleep, yet he did. He found himself in the morning being woken by his mother. It was still early and he couldn't understand how she had got there so quickly.

"We had a special speed boat to send us here. That is, I came. Your father is still in Nadi."

"My....my father. That sounds so strange."

"We're going back to the resort. I think it's time you met your father. I think it might have been better if it hadn't been in such circumstances, but that's life. I've collected Daisy's things. We are going back right away."

Chad said goodbye to Josiah and the woman who had helped him. He nearly cried because saying goodbye was saying goodbye to India forever.

They climbed aboard the speedboat and crossed the water back to the resort. Chad climbed out on to the sand and walked up to the hotel. He was afraid of meeting his dad. How could he explain his part in India's fate?

They came up to the restaurant and he could see a tall man sitting at a table with two policemen. Chad came to the table with his mother.

"The missing boy. At last!" Exclaimed one of the policemen.

"My son. Missing for too long." Said Mark.

A hand fell on his shoulder. "What about me? You missed me more didn't you dad?"

"Ah but you already know that!" He laughed. "Daisy. This....this is your mother, Eileen."

Eileen was crying and hugging herself, biting her lip, trying to say something between the tears. India began to cry and looked a bit awkward for just a moment and then ran to hug her mother.

Chad started to cry because India was crying and because she was alive. The policeman had moisture in his eyes. Mark stood and put his hand on Chad's head. "So you see, it is all ok. We got em'. We got Baldy!"

Chad had to sit down and hear what had happened. After he left India, the boat had come and Baldy had dragged India from the bure, partly as Chad had guessed, by the hair. She had put up a good fight and deliberated loosened her sandal for evidence. She knew Chad would be trying to get help.

Another man had come to shore and he tied India so that she could be carried on to the boat. He was angry with Baldy. "Too risky!" He kept saying. He was happy with turtle traffic and coral, but kidnapping was another business.

Before the dawn came, the police had reached the boat. Because Josiah had been able to give a good description and the name, they had been able to track the boat right away. The crew had been arrested and India set free to be returned to her father.

"It was a stinky, rusty old barge of a thing. They kept threatening to go to sea. I don't think they knew what to do with me. They were all arguing. That's how the police found them. Good job! I hope Baldy rots in prison!"

The police had a lot of questions. "Why did Chad recognise Baldy? What was this friendship with his uncle? Soon it was revealed. The boxes at the back of the house were full of coral. Gordon was a link in the smuggling chain. The police went and arrested him. Eileen was a bit sad but Chad was elated. Sa had already gone. She had been tired of Gordon's ways and had already gone back to her village.

"I hope I see aunt Sa again. No one makes pancakes like aunt Sa."

When Chad mentioned about the photo on the net, the police checked Baldy's records. Here was a man who made his living smuggling wildlife. In Queensland, he was wanted for smuggling rare native birds; he'd already been caught once with eggs strapped to his body as he went through customs. Now he was a failed coral smuggler. He was going to go away for a long time.

Mark said. "There's still days of Chad's holiday left. I vote we all stay here for another week. After what we have been through, we need a holiday!"

Chad noticed his mother's eyes lit with a strange light. India yelped with joy and danced around the restaurant. Chad said. "Any one can see, it was meant to be!"

Printed in Great Britain
by Amazon